Squire

with

Fire

· When Sparks Fly ·

WRITTEN & ILLUSTRATED BY

Joseph Cassis

"What are you doing up there, Grandpa?"

said Mac, as she stared up the steps of a very tall ladder. Her grandpa
pulled out a small gray safe from the top shelf in the bedroom closet.

"Grandpa, what's in that metal box?"

"Family mementos," responded Grandpa.

"WHat are MEMENTOS?"
asKed Mac.

Grandpa answered, "Oh, mementos are things that have been saved because they have special meaning, or because they remind people of events or other persons. In this case, your grandma and I saved these things to give you someday. They were handed down from your ancestors, who lived a very long time ago."

Grandpa climbed down the ladder. "This safe has an old wooden chest in it that has many treasures."

"Treasures like pirates have?" Mac asked excitedly.

"Well, kind of, but better," said Grandpa. "They belong to our family, which makes them priceless. Let's go out to the garage, Mac, since this is pretty dirty and needs some cleaning. I have several things to show you."

2

Mac and her grandpa entered the garage and walked over to the workbench with the safe. Grandpa placed it on the scuffed-up table next to the lawnmower.

Spinning the combination lock to several spots on the dial, Grandpa opened the safe and carefully took an old wooden chest out of it.

Mac eagerly climbed up on the stool next to the table so she could see inside this mysterious container.

"Those GREAT, GREAT, ancestors . . . are you talking about the KNIGHTS, SQUIRES, and SPITFIRE THE DRAGON?"

Grandpa chuckled, "Oh, so you remember my last story about Squire Mackenzie and the friendly dragon she named Spitfire who helped warm up the castle?"

"Yes, Grandpa, I do! It was a great story. And I was named after her, right?"

Grandpa took a clean rag that was hanging on a hook and wiped off the top of the chest. Dust went flying. He and Mac coughed.

"That's correct Mac. Don't you like your name, Mackenzie, or Mac, for short?"

4

Mac responded sadly, "Yes, except when people think I'm a boy."

Grandpa smiled as he advised Mac,

"Oh, don't let that bother you. Always keep people guessing so you can SURPRISE them."

"Why, Grandpa?"

"Because many people are prejudiced."

Mac was confused and asked, "What does prejudiced mean?"

Grandpa thought for a moment and then said, "Good question, Mac. It's when people are for or against someone or something before they actually get to know the person or situation. They make judgements for the wrong reasons."

Mac nodded. "Oh, that isn't good."

Mac coughed again as her grandpa waved his arms to try to scatter the fine particles hovering in the air. "I'm so sorry, Mackenzie. I didn't realize there was so much dust that piled up on this chest," Grandpa said, as they choked on the cloud of dust.

"What's in there, Grandpa? Let's see the treasure," said Mac.

Grandpa slowly lifted the top. The hinges creaked very loudly. "Needs some oil, huh? We have to be careful with this chest. It's very old."

Mac nodded again.

"I'm so excited," she said. "Let's see what's in there." Mac tapped her hands several times on her thighs with eagerness.

Grandpa pulled out some crinkled old parchment with drawings on it.

"WHAT'S THAT, GRANDPA?"

asked Mac.

"Oh, these are actual drawings of a map drawn on parchment, which is the specially prepared very thin skin of a sheep or a goat. Parchment was used during ancient and medieval times like we use paper made from wood."

"Grandpa, this is so exciting. May I see the map?"

"The parchments are very fragile and can easily tear. Here, hold very carefully, Mac."

Mac slowly reached for the very old map and held it gently. She looked at all the lines, circles, and other shapes, as well as unusual words written on the parchment.

"What does all this mean?" she asked.

Grandpa pointed to the map and explained, "The map has special markings that shows where your ancestors buried their swords and shields in case there was danger."

"Wow! Where are the swords and shields buried? We should go to Scotland and find them, right, Grandpa?"

"Excellent, Mac. You remembered that your ancestors lived in Scotland. Maybe someday we'll travel there and see if those swords and shields still exist." Grandpa said this as he cautiously took the parchment back from Mac and placed it into the chest. Mac saw something else in the box.

"What's that, Grandpa?"

"Oh, that's a bag of marbles. It's an ancient game going back thousands of years," explained Grandpa, as he pulled a purple cloth bag from the chest.

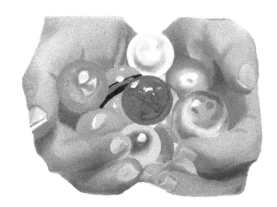

"They used rocks that were smoothed into small balls by the rushing river water. Later in history, marbles were made from glass. The players would make a circle on the ground and then try to hit the marbles out of it."

Grandpa took a couple of the beautiful, colorful glass marbles out of the bag and handed one to Mac. He bent down and drew a circle on the dusty garage floor.

Then Grandpa placed six marbles in the middle of the circle. Each was clear like glass, but had different colors inside.

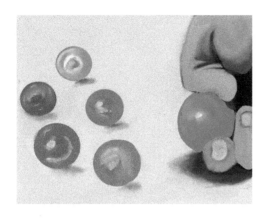

As Grandpa went down on his knees, he told Mac, "Try to hit the center marbles out of the circle with your 'shooter' marble, which is the big marble like this." He carefully aimed the larger marble by holding his thumb against the shooter marble while balancing it on top of his thumb. He released this shiny marble with a quick flick of his thumb.

The shooter marble rolled fast toward the center of the circle. It hit three smaller marbles and knocked them out of the circle.

"Wow, Grandpa, that's amazing. You're really good!"

Grandpa collected all of the marbles and placed them back into the center of the circle.

"Normally, each person tries to get as many marbles knocked out of the circle as they can. Those with the most knocked out wins the game. There are many other games you can play, too. But, for now, let's just try shooting the marbles."

Grandpa handed the shooter marble to Mac. "Now you try it, Mac," he said.

Mackenzie went down on her knees and held her marble like Grandpa had shown her. She released her shooter and it rolled quickly to the center, but with less force. Three marbles were hit and they moved a few inches out of the circle.

"I DID IT!
I Hit the other
marbles!!

screamed Mac.

"That's excellent, Mackenzie, especially for your very first shot. To be good, you have to keep practicing. I had a lot of practice in my day. It's so much fun when you build confidence knowing you can aim, shoot and hit with lots of force."

"So did Squire Mackenzie know how to play with these marbles?" asked Mac.

"Oh, yes, exactly. That's how the squires and knights learned ways to beat their opponents.

The game showed them how to think and be creative to win. It was called battle planning. Let's put these away for now and see what else is in the box."

"OK. The marble game is really fun, Grandpa, said Mac. Grandpa and Mac collected the marbles and placed them back into the bag. Mac peeked into the wooden box again.

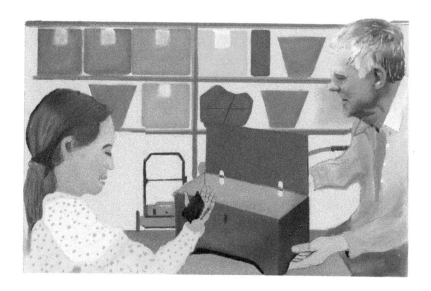

"There's more. What is this? Why are you saving these old rocks and that piece of metal?" she asked.

They aren't just any old rocks, Mac. They make fire," exclaimed Grandpa.

"No way, Grandpa. Rocks don't make fire! You have to use a match or a lighter."

Grandpa responded, "That's also true, but knights and squires didn't have matches or lighters back 600 years ago."

"That's so funny, Grandpa. What, you hit the rocks together and, ka-boom, there is instant fire? That's so funny," Mac chuckled.

"That's true, too, Mac!" Grandpa laughed at Mac's surprise.

"What? No way, Grandpa. I was only kidding," roared Mac.

"Well, I'm not. I'll show you, but we have to go out into the yard." Grandpa grabbed the small rocks and the piece of metal.

"Let's go!" he said, and motioned Mac to follow him out the door.

Grandpa went into the garage and came back with two pairs of safety goggles. He placed one on his head covering his eyes and handed the other to Mac. "Please put these on to protect your eyes," he said.

"The Knights and Squires had goggles, too?" asked Mac.

"No, silly, but we know now how pieces of rock can get chipped off and possibly fly up into your eyes. You don't want to lose your eyesight, do you?"

"NO WAY!"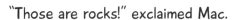

shouted Mac.

"And, remember, don't you play with matches, lighters, or even these 'cherts,'" said Grandpa.

"Those are rocks!" exclaimed Mac.

"Well, these aren't just any old rocks. They are called cherts or flints, and were very plentiful in the area in Scotland where Squire Mackenzie and your other ancestors lived. When you strike a chert with another chert or, better yet, a piece of metal, sparks will fly and you can start a fire," explained Grandpa.

"I didn't know that, Grandpa," said Mac.

"The fire builder aims the shooting sparks next to some tinder or small shavings of wood or very small twigs."

Grandpa sternly reminded Mac, "Be careful when doing this, especially anytime you are working with fire, or else you can get burned very badly or possibly burn down something like your house. Understand?"

Mac shook her head up and down several times. "Yes, Grandpa. I promise."

With that, Grandpa struck the rock sharply with the metal rod and sparks shot out.

"Wow, Grandpa!! That IS AMAZING!"

"Where's Spitfire when you need him?" asked Grandpa, laughing.

"Yep," said Mac, giggling. "That dragon would simply aim his fiery breath at some logs and blow a flame on them to start a fire.

"Like in that story you told me where the dragon would aim his fiery breath and heat that big kettle."

"Yes, but when you don't have a dragon around, you have to rely upon your chert. That's what the other knights and squires had to use to make a fire. "OK, now let's try it again near some of these dried-up leaves," said Grandpa as he collected some leaves and placed them to form a pile.

He struck the rock again and sparks hit the pile of leaves.

Grandpa gently blew on the leaves and smoke started to bellow. He quickly placed some twigs on the pile and blew on it again. The smoke ignited into a small fire.

"There you go! We have a small fire. Mac, you've got to promise me not to play with fire or try to start a fire without your parents or me around to be sure all goes well. OK?" Grandpa sternly warned his granddaughter again.

"I promise, Grandpa, but you said the squires built fires and they were only seven years old like me, remember?"

"Yes, but the young squires always had their older squires or knights near them," explained Grandpa.

"Really? I will be careful and won't do it by myself. I remember Billy's dad accidently burned down their house when he fell asleep smoking a cigarette," said Mac.

"Oh, no. That is so sad. Did anyone get hurt?" Grandpa frowned.

"No. Everyone was safe. By the way, I did learn how to start campfires in scouting, but we only used matches . . . not rocks!"

Grandpa was pleased to hear that Mac understood. "Very good. Yes, fire can be very dangerous, but it is also good for heating our homes, making engines in our cars work, cooking our food. OK, enough. Now you know how the knights and squires made fire to keep warm and cook their food when they traveled.

"Thanks, Grandpa, for showing me. That was amazing," said Mac.

"There you go, Mac. Now, let me tell you what you must know about your ancestors and what they did to live and survive."

"That would be great, Grandpa. Maybe you can help me with my school report. Mrs. Akre assigned our class to pick a country where one or more of our relatives lived. Any ideas?"

"Oh, yes, I have a few," said Grandpa, and grinned a big smile.

"Did I ever tell you about how Squire Mackenzie and Spitfire stopped an invasion of their castle by Vikings?"

"No, I don't think so.

WHat's an INVASION?"

Grandpa turned to Mac, held out the cherts, and said, "That's when bad people attack or fight good people to take over their place or steal things from them. These rocks or cherts belonged to your ancestor, Mackenzie Stewart, who was a knight. Before being a knight, she was a strong squire and actually saved the castle from being overtaken by Vikings who invaded the land."

"So, what happened to Squire Mackenzie and Spitfire?" asked Mac.

"Let's go into the house and I'll show you."

Grandpa and Mac walked back into the house with the cherts and the metal rod. They sat down on the floor.

"Before being a knight, she was a strong squire and actually saved the castle from being overtaken by Vikings who invaded the land," explained Grandpa.

"VIKINGS? WHO are THey?"

"Vikings came from the area now known as Denmark, Sweden, and Norway. These warriors were also known as Norsemen, but women were Vikings, too. The Vikings controlled Scotland, where those cherts came from near the Rothesay Castle."

Grandpa pointed toward the cherts now lying on some magazines.

"Oh, I remember that castle from the first story about Squire Mackenzie and Spitfire."

Grandpa continued. "So, the Vikings surrounded the castle and were about to attack to control the village and surrounding area."

"But Spitfire will save them, right?" asked Mac.

"Squire Mackenzie and Spitfire were out in the forest. They didn't know these invaders were about to storm the castle," said Grandpa.

yelled Mac.

"Yes, big trouble, Mac. The Vikings got their large ramming log and lined up on the bridge after crossing the moat. They were going to pound the log against the huge, thick doors protecting the castle's entrance."

Mac continued to be surprised and asked, "Why wasn't the bridge up so the Vikings couldn't cross the moat to go through the doors?"

Grandpa continued telling his story. "The Vikings had waited until dark and snuck up to the bridge without being spotted by the castle guards. When the castle guards saw them in the morning, it was too late. They started to bring up the bridge, but because there were so many Vikings on it, the guards could not lift it up to protect the castle from invasion.

"The Viking mob would strike the door several times. The powerful vibrations would shatter the wood and loosen the big bolts holding the timbers together.

"Most of the Vikings were lined up on the bridge to rush into the castle once the doors broke open. Just about when it looked like the doors were about to burst open, a loud cry could be heard.

RHeeeee!

and Spitfire came swooping down blowing fire across the group of Vikings. They immediately tried to scatter, knowing Spitfire was turning around in flight to blow more fire at them. Many Vikings bumped into each other. Some lost their balance and fell into the moat where snakes and snapping turtles bit them. Those Vikings screamed, 'Ooeeee...yowl.'

"Meanwhile, Mackenzie had snuck up to the bridge and built a fire line, which was made up of hay from the nearby hay stokes along with tree branches."

Mac was fascinated with the story and asked, "Grandpa, why didn't the Vikings see Squire Mackenzie build the fire line?"

"Great question, Mac. They didn't because all the Vikings were so focused on breaking down the big doors. They did not look behind them or have a lookout Viking watching to ensure they were safe. Meanwhile, Spitfire was busy blowing fire on the Vikings."

Mac smiled and said, "She is so smart."

Grandpa continued: "Then, just like I showed you, she took out her chert, or 'fire rock,' and struck it with a metal rod. A big spark lit the hay on fire. She blew on the flame and the fire followed the path of the fire line, forming a huge fire wall that was about six feet tall and trapped the Vikings on the bridge."

"Did the bridge catch on fire?" asked Mac.

"No, Squire Mackenzie was smart and did not want to burn down the bridge. She built the fire line several feet in front of the bridge entrance. Meanwhile, Spitfire had enough time to come back, flying over the Vikings and breathing more fire on them.

"Oh, didn't the snakes and snapping turtles in the moat bite them?" asked Mac.

"Yes, it was either fighting off the snakes and turtles or burning to death by Spitfire's **Fiery breath**."

Mac quickly responded, "Yes, I would probably fight off the snakes and turtles, but I don't like snakes. They scare me!"

Grandpa chuckled. "Me, too! I don't like snakes, but many snakes are not mean or poisonous. In fact, some are milked for their venom or poison to make powerful drugs for humans."

Surprised to learn this about snakes, Mac asked, "So they are like people—some are good and others are not so good?"

"Yes, Mac, you have to be careful and always be alert or you can get into trouble."

Mac shook her head and said, "Like Sally, who was approached by a bad guy in a van. She ran home because she thought he was a bad person. My mom and one of my teachers always remind me, saying, "stranger danger!"

Grandpa said, "Yes, very good to know. Yet, there are many people who come to the aid of strangers. In that case, they are good strangers. Just trust your instincts and always be smart."

Mac responded, "Like Mackenzie. She saw a chance to save the day by trapping the Vikings so that Spitfire could scare them away, right, Grandpa?"

"Exactly. Spitfire scared them so much the Vikings even ran through the fire wall to escape the possibility of Spitfire coming back to burn them to death.

"Meanwhile, the guards in the castle had opened up one of the two doors to come out to fight the Vikings who were either thinking of jumping off the bridge or running through the fire wall to escape the battle. The Vikings were overrun by the guards with the help of Spitfire. Those that remained decided to jump through the firewall and darted back into the woods.

"Squire Mackenzie told Spitfire, 'Follow the Vikings and keep blowing fire on them until they go far away from the castle.' Spitfire nodded and flew after the Vikings.

"Then, suddenly, Spitfire got hit with an arrow and fell to the ground."

"**OH NO, WHat HappeNed to SpitFire!?**" asked Mac.

Grandpa saw that Mac was extremely sad and quickly told her the great and amazing news. "He and the villagers were saved by another dragon called Sparky!! Meanwhile, the nearby villagers took the arrow out of Spitfire's wing and applied medicine as Sparky flew around them for protection from the Vikings."

"Yeah, Spitfire. Glad he was rescued. So, Sparky is another dragon?" Mac asked excitedly. "Wow, where did he come from?"

"Sparky was a girl dragon. She was flying by the castle and wanted to meet Spitfire. She had heard he was doing great things to help the village and Mackenzie's castle. Sparky thought this was what she wanted to do, too. Other castles were hunting down dragons and she was scared that she would be next. Fortunately, she saw the fighting that was going on. She also saw Spitfire needing help and went to his aid."

"Great!

THe CaStLe WaS SaVed by MacKeNzie aNd SpitFire,"

exclaimed Mac.

"And Sparky—don't forget her," said Grandpa. "Yes, in fact, Squire Mackenzie told Spitfire she'd never seen him looking so mean. Spitfire told her in dragon language, 'I had to be mean because those Vikings were after everyone in the castle. Those people are my family and I must protect my family.'"

"They probably didn't have time to have s'mores, right?" asked Mac giggling.

Grandpa laughed. "That's funny, Mac. You remembered how I teased you with Squire Mackenzie and Spitfire having s'mores. Unfortunately, they didn't have them back in those days."

Mac quickly responded, "Yes, I remembered from the first story about Mackenzie and Spitfire. Too bad! I loved those s'mores!"

"Yes, me too! Having s'mores would have been a great way to celebrate the team effort. Squire Mackenzie used a battle plan she remembered from playing those marbles. Mackenzie also remembered her training on how to start a fire with her fire rock and metal rod."

Mac added to Grandpa's observation. "Yes, Mackenzie is so clever. She remembered how to use those cherts to start her fire."

"But the trouble hadn't stopped. The Vikings came back to fight again, even though there were two dragons protecting the castle," explained Grandpa.

"OH MY GOSH.

Did the Vikings hurt or kill Mackenzie and the people in the castle?"

Grandpa calmly continued the story. "Actually, Squire Mackenzie told the attacking Vikings to stop as she laid down her sword. They were stunned. She told them that it made no sense to attack the castle again and try to kill everyone. The villagers were the ones who would be supplying the Vikings with food and clothing, and not just once, but for a long time."

"Why would she put her sword down on the ground?" asked Mac. "Was she crazy? The dragons were going to protect Mackenzie and all the villagers, right?"

Grandpa responded, "Exactly. Mackenzie knew the dragons would protect them, but if they were to continue to battle and even win, many people—Vikings, knights, squires, and villagers—would get hurt or, worse, be killed."

"But how did she convince the Vikings to stop fighting?" asked Mac.

"Odin, the Viking leader was stunned to see this type of thinking," explained Grandpa. "Squire Mackenzie challenged Odin to three games of marbles. Odin agreed, but only if they would play three games of *Hnefatafl*. If the Vikings won, the castle would have to provide food and clothing to the Vikings for two years. If Mackenzie won, the Vikings would not attack the castle

...Forever."

"Very smart of Mackenzie. What is the *Neffa-thingy* game?"

"Hnefatafl, pronounced 'neffa-taffle,' was also known as 'the King's Table.'"

"It's a funny name, neffa-taffle," Mac said, and laughed. "So, it's like Mackenzie's marble game, right?"

Grandpa clarified, "Not exactly. Many people considered the game as the greatest board game in history. It was the Vikings' game of strategy. The pieces are set out on the board with the king piece on the center square, his defenders around him, and the attackers at each edge of the board."

"Instead of a king, could it be a queen?" asked Mac.

"Well, yes, the Vikings would set up the game the way they wanted to pretend who they may attack in real life," explained Grandpa.

"So, Who Won?"

"Squire Mackenzie, of course! She won all three marble games because she practiced so many times. She won the last game of Hnefatafl, giving her the highest total score. Mackenzie was a quick learner."

Just then, Joyce, Mackenzie's mom, came into the living room from the garage.

"Hi, Dad and Mackenzie. How are you doing? Hey, what are those rocks doing in the living room!?" she asked.

Mac explained, "They aren't just any rocks, Mom. They are fire rocks, called cherts or flints!"

"I'm sorry, my little rock collectors, but please take those rocks, or whatever you called them, outside, where they belong," Joyce sternly stated.

"Now, my dear daughter, Joyce, be cool," said Grandpa calmly. "I placed them on a pile of magazines so they wouldn't scratch the floor. I was telling Mac how our ancestors used them to build fires to live."

Mackenzie's mom immediately looked back at Grandpa.

"Oh, great. Now you're teaching her how to start fires!"

Mac immediately said, "No, Mom, I'm not going to start fires. Besides, they teach us in scouting how to build a campfire. You never know when a person may need to know this."

"That's right, Mackenzie," said Grandpa.

Joyce answered, "I know you are a very responsible person, so I trust you will always do the right thing."

"I will, Mom. Like Grandpa says, 'I need to follow the same rules as Squire Mackenzie did.' Oh, and be as creative by playing marbles and Hnefatafl."

"What? Playing marbles and Naffa-what?" asked Joyce.

Grandpa and Mackenzie laughed. Mackenzie quickly responded. "It's a Viking game called Hnefatafl," she said. "Funny name huh? And the knights and squires played marbles made from round rocks."

Mom responded with smile, "Well, that's much better than playing with fire."

Mac chuckled. "You can only win when you practice . . . lots of practice."

THE END — Let's play marbles!

Dedicated to Joyce,
the spark in my life.

FriesenPress

Suite 300 - 990 Fort St
Victoria, BC, V8V 3K2
Canada

www.friesenpress.com

Compenso Creations, Inc.
6505 NW 97th Street
Johnston, Iowa 50131

www.compensocreations.com

Feedback and fan information, please visit www.squirewithfire.com

Ordering Information:
Special discounts are available on quantity purchases by corporations, associations, educators, and other organizations. For details, please contact the publisher and/or author at the above-listed addresses.

ISBN
978-1-5255-6349-2 (Hardcover)
978-1-5255-6350-8 (Paperback)
978-1-5255-6351-5 (eBook)

1. JUVENILE FICTION, FAIRY TALES & FOLKLORE

Distributed to the trade by The Ingram Book Company

CPSIA information can be obtained
at www.ICGtesting.com
Printed in the USA
BVHW022121300120
571016BV00001B/1

9 781525 563492

BE POSITIVE!

THIS BOOK BELONGS TO

_____

WELCOME TO BE POSITIVE!

Author
DR. SHARIE COOMBES
Child and Family Psychotherapist

We all feel like we don't measure up from time to time and this fun activity book is a great way to get you thinking and talking about the things that bother you, so you can get on with being the real, amazing you and get back to enjoying life.

Doing these activities will help you to feel more positive and self-assured, understand and combat your negative feelings, learn about and improve your self-esteem and confidence and talk to others about your worries (if you want to). You could use this book in a quiet, comfortable place where you can think and feel relaxed and it's up to you which pages you do. You might do a page a day if that's what you want to do, or complete lots of pages in one go. You can start anywhere in the book and even come back to a page many times. There are no rules!

Sometimes we can feel so stuck that we start to believe nothing will help but there is always a solution to every problem. Nothing is so big that it can't be sorted out or talked about even if it feels that way. You could show some of these activities to important people in your life to help explain how you are feeling and to get help with what is upsetting you. You can always talk to an adult you trust at school or ask an adult at home to take you to the doctor for support to sort out any problems.

Lots of children need a bit of extra help every now and then, and here are three organisations you can turn to if you don't want to talk to people you know. They have helped thousands of children with every kind of problem and will know how to help you. They won't be shocked by what you tell them, however bad it feels to you.

CHILDLINE

Help and advice about a wide range of issues.

Comforts, advises and protects children 24 hours a day and offers free confidential counselling by helpline, online chat and Ask Sam.

Tel: 0800 1111   www.childline.org.uk

YOUNG MINDS

Mental health and wellbeing information, advice and help for young people.

Provides information on the website and a crisis text-line available 24/7 across the UK if you are experiencing a mental health crisis.

Texts are free from EE, 02, Vodafone, 3, Virgin Mobile, BT Mobile, GiffGaff, Tesco Mobile and Telecom Plus.

Text YM to: 85258
www.youngminds.org.uk

THE SAMARITANS

Listening and support for anyone who needs it.

Contact 24 hours a day, 365 days a year – calls and emails are free and confidential. If you need a response immediately, it's best to call on the phone.

Email: jo@samaritans.org
Tel: 116 123 (24 hours)   www.samaritans.org

BIGGER, BRAVER, STRONGER, SMARTER

Growing up is exciting!

Every day, you learn or discover something new about yourself and the world and you can try new things you couldn't do before.

Sometimes, growing up also feels challenging. Family, friends and teachers ask more from you. You get bigger, braver, stronger and smarter – and so do your friends. You all do this in your own way and in your own time.

Your friends will have different strengths and talents to you.

It's a fact of life that no-one's perfect or talented at everything and no-one is positive all the time. Sometimes you'll have sad, angry, frustrated, worried and other negative feelings. When these show up, it's good to recognise them, notice why they've surfaced and be kind to yourself. But it's important to make sure they don't stick around for too long.

Your brilliant body experiences a huge range of feelings every day as a result of the emotions that blast off in nanoseconds in your brain, because of what it sees, feels, thinks and believes.

LOOK OUT FOR THE THINKING POINTS THROUGHOUT THE BOOK. THESE ARE IDEAS FOR YOU TO THINK ABOUT FURTHER, OR DISCUSS WITH A FRIEND OR ADULT.

Learning to **BE POSITIVE!** will improve your:

SELF-ESTEEM

SELF-CONFIDENCE

BODY IMAGE

WORLD VIEW

Your brain works astronomically hard to keep up with your growing body, sometimes making you feel clumsy or uncomfortable and affecting the way you see yourself and the world around you.

Don't worry, it's normal to lose a bit of confidence and feel unsure about yourself for a while.

UNDER CONSTRUCTION!

As you deliberately notice the good things all around you, you'll rewire your brain to Be Positive! more often. This book was written to give you loads of ideas about how to do this and how to feel better.

Imagine how great you're going to feel now you can **BE POSITIVE!**

YOU'VE GOT THE POWER!

Fill in and colour the countdown to get started!

10 9 8

YOU'VE GOT THE POWER

How positive do you feel right now?

Here are some words or phrases that are used throughout the book.

Read the definition and then colour each battery to show if you're feeling negative, positive or somewhere in between. Start at the negative end and colour until you reach your personal power point.

SELF-ESTEEM

How you view yourself as a person and what you feel, think and believe about yourself and about how others think of you. What you believe about your value to others and the world around you and what you deserve from them.

NEGATIVE
I'm rubbish, I get everything wrong

POSITIVE
I make mistakes but I learn from them and keep trying

SELF-CONFIDENCE

How you act in the world because of what you see, feel, think and believe about yourself.

NEGATIVE
I don't like to try new things

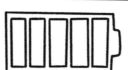

POSITIVE
I love a new challenge

BODY IMAGE

How you see your body and appearance and what you feel, think and believe about these and about how others see them.

NEGATIVE
I always
look dreadful

POSITIVE
This jumper
really suits me

WORLD VIEW

How you expect things to work out in your life and in the world around you.

NEGATIVE
I bet I lose
the game

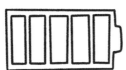

POSITIVE
If I play my best,
I might win

You can build up your Be Positive! power.

Come back and update this page every time you feel a shift upwards!

Doing more of the activities in this book will boost it even further.

BODY TALK

Where in your body do you notice negative feelings?

Draw on this picture to show how it makes you feel and where you feel it. You can use the suggested feelings or make up your own.

Remember or imagine having to do something difficult when your confidence is low and you feel uncomfortable and negative. What is it?

_____

_____

FIZZY   JUMPY   TINGLY   FLUTTERY   FAINT   SHY

SICK   CONFUSED   DIZZY   NERVOUS   CLAMMY

SHAKY   HOT   NUMB   EMBARRASSED   TIGHT

No wonder you feel negative with all these tricky sensations in your body.

Let's rewire your brain to **BE POSITIVE!**

SEPARATE   CLUMSY   SWEATY   COLD   AWKWARD

Remember or imagine having to do something difficult when your confidence is high and you feel proud and positive. What is it?

⬇

_____

_____

Draw on this picture to show how it makes you feel and where you feel it. You can use the suggested feelings or make up your own.

⬇

COURAGEOUS

SATISFIED

COMFORTABLE

HAPPY

PEACEFUL

CALM

CAPABLE

CURIOUS

CONFIDENT

FANTASTIC

CHEERFUL

PROUD

EXCITED

GIGGLY   BOLD

INTERESTED

DELIGHTED

BUZZY   ENERGETIC

AMUSED

Look back at your negative picture and remember or imagine that time again. Keep thinking about that time while you look at this positive picture and carry on until you feel confident about that old situation.

WELL DONE – you've just rewired your brain to Be Positive! You've got this and next time, it will be easier to Be Positive!

THINKING POINT:

What is the difference when you are confident? How does it change your experience? Try explaining this to a friend or adult or write about it if you want to.

EYE MATTER

Our eyes are windows to who we are and how we're feeling. Everyone's eyes are different – get to know yours by looking at them closely in a mirror.

Notice the colours, shapes, patterns, lashes, sparkle and shine of your eyes.

Draw and colour them here:

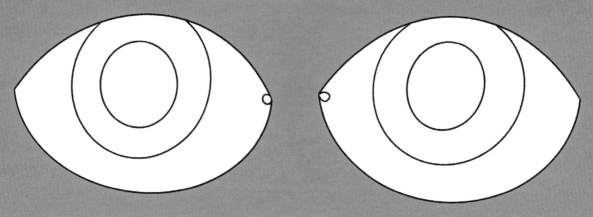

Making eye contact with others helps us to be and feel understood.

Ask someone else to sit still in front of you so that you can get to know their eyes and then draw them with the same attention to detail.

If you prefer, you could use a photograph of a person or animal instead.

See if you can work out how they are feeling by the look in their eyes.

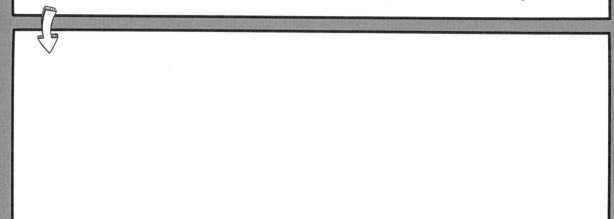

SNAZZY SHADES

Colour these snazzy shades however you like and use them to protect your eyes from negativity for a confidence boost.

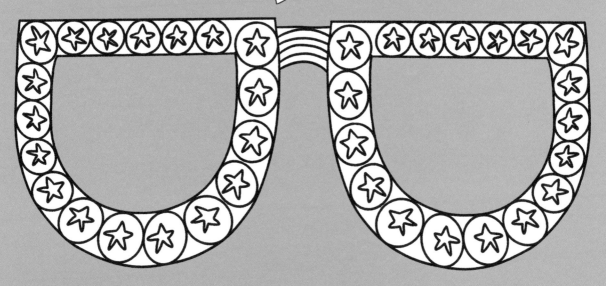

Why not cut them out and try them on for size?

Use a pencil to push out the lenses so you can see.

Ask an adult to help if needed.

Use tape to stick the arms to the frames.

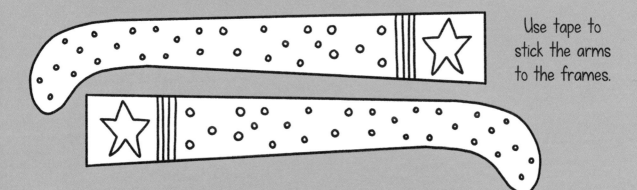

Remember a time you felt down about yourself and try to recall how you saw the world around you then. Now go back to that time and imagine putting on your shades to see how they change the way you feel about yourself and how you act.

Next time you're feeling low, imagine putting on these shades, as you feel and act more confident.

GET CHANGED

What big or little changes have
happened to you recently?

Make a list here and colour the
▭ if it was a negative change or
✚ if it was a positive change.
Some changes might be both.

HOME

SCHOOL

LOST
SOMETHING
OR SOMEONE

PET

CLASS

GROWN OUT
OF YOUR
FAVOURITE
SHOES

CLUB

FRIEND

POSITIVE

Pick one of your positive
changes and say how it has
made things better for you.

Now pick one of your negative
changes – let's work out how you
can flip it and make it feel more
positive. What help do you need?
Who can help you?

NEGATIVE

YOU'RE INCREDIBLE!

Ask your friends and family what they find special about you and write their thoughts here.

Add your own ideas to the list too.

Fill in these rosettes with the special strengths and qualities you're most proud of from the list.

Write the name of the person who said it on the ribbon.

KIND AND CARING

A GOOD LISTENER

TELLS FUNNY JOKES

Award yourself all these medals in an imaginary ceremony. Make sure you notice how proud the audience members are and how loudly they are cheering for you.

WORLD VIEW

What's your world view?

Colour the world however you want to.

THINKING POINT:

Did you know your world view is influenced by:

• Your family's world view

• Your cultural background

• Experiences you've had

• Your close relationships

Use this telescope to focus in on the detail of your own incredible personal world.

Fill it with words or pictures of all the good things and people in your life.

MY INCREDIBLE WORLD IS FULL OF WONDERFUL THINGS AND PEOPLE

THIS IS ME!

Take a bit of me-time!

Draw yourself looking exactly how you want the world to see you.

Perhaps you're doing something you love, or striking a fun pose!

Notice how good you feel about yourself when you're seen for who you really are.

What would you like to hear other people say about you?

Write these things all over the page if you like.

KIND MIND

A kind mind can help you focus on what's positive in your life, see things differently and improve your self-esteem and confidence.

TRY IT OUT!

Do you tell yourself negative things?

Do you blame yourself for things?

Is it hard to think you did well or deserve nice things?

If so, you need to learn how to speak more kindly to yourself.

I'm having a difficult day → My friend is coming over for tea later

I'm rubbish at_____ → I'm great at _____

I don't like my _____ → I like my _____

_____ → _____

_____ → _____

_____ → _____

_____ → _____

Next time you think something negative about yourself, call up your kind mind and turn things around.

Your kind mind has already rewired your brain to notice the positive things in the future – keep practising!

LUCKY STARS

Fill in these lucky stars with the things and people you feel thankful to have in your life.

FRIENDS

COMFY BED

Unkindness may happen and things will sometimes go wrong, but with your positive power and people to support you, you can be confident and happy!

SPACE RACE

UP FOR A CHALLENGE?

Take each rocket on a space journey using one long scribble without taking your pen or pencil off the page. You decide where the journey stops.

BONUS! When you've flown all your rockets, colour in any cool patterns you've made.

REACH FOR THE STARS!

Whenever things aren't going well or you need a confidence boost, reach for the stars.

Your body will enjoy the challenge and you'll feel more positive in no time!

Play some music if you like, to give yourself a beat to move to.

STARBURSTS

Stretch your hands up high above your head and hold your fists shut.

Open and close your fists 30 times, as fast as possible. Keep both hands in time with each other or alternate them.

STAR TURNS

Stand with your feet slightly apart and your arms stretched up and out so you look like a star. Take your right hand and put it onto your left foot. Straighten up again. Now take your left hand and put it onto your right foot. Straighten up.

Carry on like this for a whole minute!

STAR JUMPS

Now go back to standing with your feet slightly apart and your arms stretched out like a star. Jump up and, as you land, bring your feet together with your hands on your hips. Jump up again and go back into your star shape.

Repeat and see if you can keep going for two minutes.

Put a tick in a box each time you complete one of the activities.

STARBURSTS									
STAR TURNS									
STAR JUMPS									

ALIEN FRIENDS

This alien is a long way from home and everything here looks strange.

 Colour it in and draw some friends for the alien to hang out with.

What is it about YOU that would make them want to be friends with you?

ROCKET MISSION

Mistakes make you learn faster and go further, like a rocket.

Fill these rockets with mistakes you've made that helped your brain get stronger.

Add extra rockets if you want to.

Forgot something important - made me more organised

Lifting weights makes your muscles stronger. Your brain is like a muscle and gets stronger and smarter every time you make a mistake.

THINKING POINT:

How did these mistakes make your brain stronger and smarter. Write it in or talk it through with someone if you want.

BREATHE POSITIVE

If your positivity needs a quick boost, try these breathing exercises to help you feel more confident.

Let your body show you how amazing it is – and how amazing you are.

3:5 BREATHING

This works wherever you are and whatever you are doing. The best bit is no-one will know you're doing it so if you need to boost your inner positivity without being noticed, give it a go.

If you want to, you could close your eyes while you do it.

Get comfortable in a sitting position.

Notice your body breathing in and out.

After a few breaths, start to count along with yourself, making your in-breath last for the count of three and your out-breath last for the count of five, breathing smoothly.

Keep going for as long you want to or until you feel great.

POWERFUL HANDS

Pick a quiet, calm spot and lie down.

Close your eyes and picture yourself in a lovely, cosy place.

Breathe deeply and slowly.

Now, focus all your attention on your hands and imagine you are warming them up.

Notice your hands start to actually feel warmer.

When you've mastered this skill, try spreading the warm feeling up your arms and down into your tummy. You'll be feeling positive and confident in no time!

FINGER BREATHING

This is a really 'handy' skill! Spread your hand out on your knee or a table.

If you prefer, you can use the picture of the hand. Notice your body breathing in and out.

Take your pointer finger from the opposite hand, put it on the bottom knuckle of your thumb and slowly trace up to the tip, breathing in as you do. Stop at the top, hold your breath for a second, then trace back down the other side while you breathe out.

Keep going until you've traced every finger in the same way smoothly. Remember to keep your breathing smooth too.

Repeat this six times, and make sure all your attention is on your hand and your breath.

ME, MYSELF & I

You are more than what you look like or what you can do.

Complete these sentences by writing things that you feel, think or believe about yourself.

I'm afraid of

_____

I have a natural talent for

_____

I can't stand

_____

I'm loved by

_____

I feel good when

_____

I'm interested in

_____

I feel frustrated when

_____

I don't believe in

_____

I'm good at

_____

I worry about

_____

I'm proud of myself for

_____

If you want to, you could try to decide more things that you think, feel and believe.

SCORES ON THE DOORS

These doors will open up your self-esteem.

Write your scores on the doors anywhere from 0 to 7.

I BELIEVE IN MYSELF

I DESERVE TO BE HAPPY

I CAN SAY WHAT I'M GOOD AT

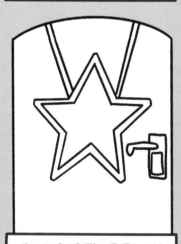

I'M IMPORTANT TO MY FRIENDS AND FAMILY

I'M PROUD OF WHAT I CAN DO

PEOPLE LISTEN TO MY IDEAS

Test your friends and family and check their self-esteem scores.

Keep doing more of these activities then come back and try again to see if your scores go up. Talk to an adult to work out how to improve your scores if they are low.

WRONG IS ALRIGHT

Make deliberate mistakes all over this page and don't rub them out.

If you accidentally make a mistake, that's even better!

$$3 + 3 = 8$$

BE POISTIVE

WRONG IS ALL WRITE

Be as creative as you can be!

You could show this page to friends and see if they can spot the mistakes – but don't change them!

STAR AS YOU ARE

Your brain is full of star-shaped cells so you're already a star as you are.

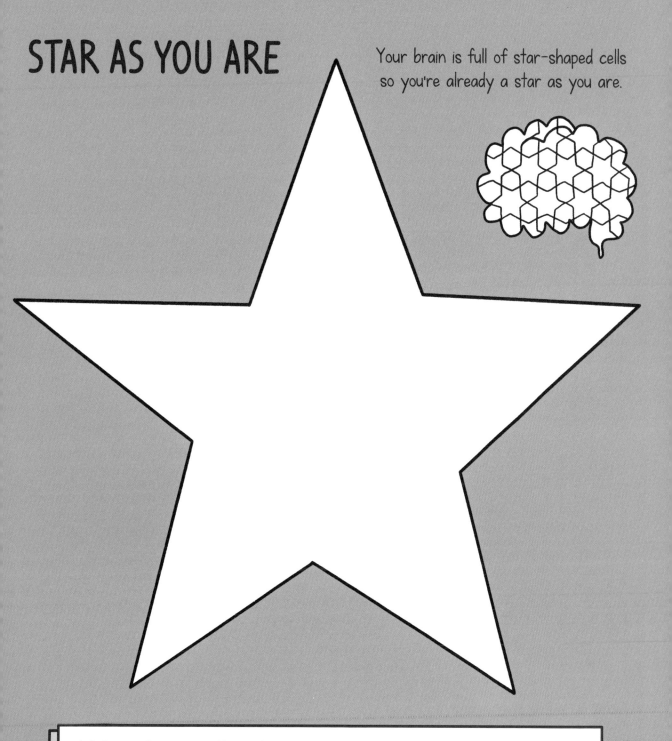

Write or draw something about you or something you've done that you're proud of in this star and add colour and patterns if you want to.

JAZZY JAR OF JOY

Want to capture some joyful feelings?

Why not make a jar of joy?

You will need: a jar with a lid, some small strips of paper, pens, glue, stickers, magazine pictures, buttons, sequins or anything fancy that you would like to decorate the jar with.

The world is full of beautiful things

Life can be great

I can and I will

Happy days ahead

I am loved

Write 31 joyful messages - you could ask your friends and family to help. Fold up the strips of paper and pop them in the jar.

Take out a joyful message whenever you need a smile and read it to yourself out loud three times.

Why not start every day by picking out a joyful message and inviting your family to join in? Making it a daily activity will rewire your brain to **BE POSITIVE!**

COLOUR THIS IN!

LIST ALL THE PEOPLE, PETS AND THINGS YOU ARE IMPORTANT TO:

I AM IMPORTANT

TRUE COLOURS

Fill in the blanks on these pages to let the world know what makes you feel different things, what you do and who you really are. You could even show them to people you trust.

_____

makes me smile.

_____

makes me frustrated.

_____

makes me laugh.

_____

makes me cry.

_____

makes me delighted.

_____

makes me furious.

_____

makes me happy.

_____

makes me sad.

I never

_____

I rarely

_____

I sometimes

_____

I often

_____

I always

_____

I used to

_____

I might

_____

I'm going to

_____

NAMES IN THE FRAMES

When people make you feel great, you should spend as much time as you can with them.

Fill these frames with whoever makes you feel great!

Write their name under their picture and add a positive comment about each one.

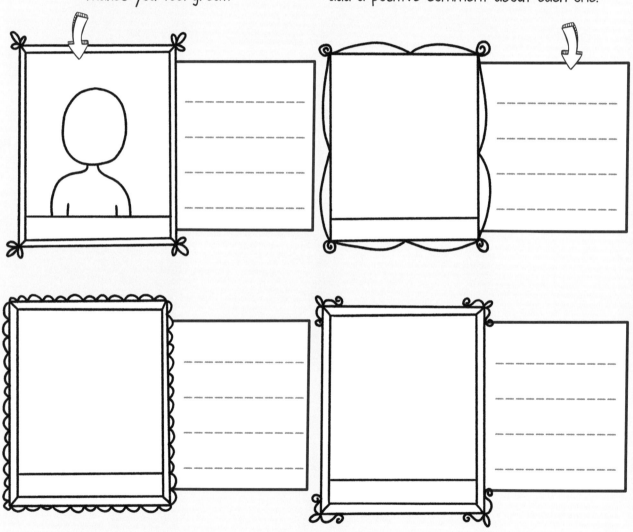

Remember to include people from all parts of your life, like family, pets, school, clubs...

Write a letter to someone who has helped you **BE POSITIVE!**

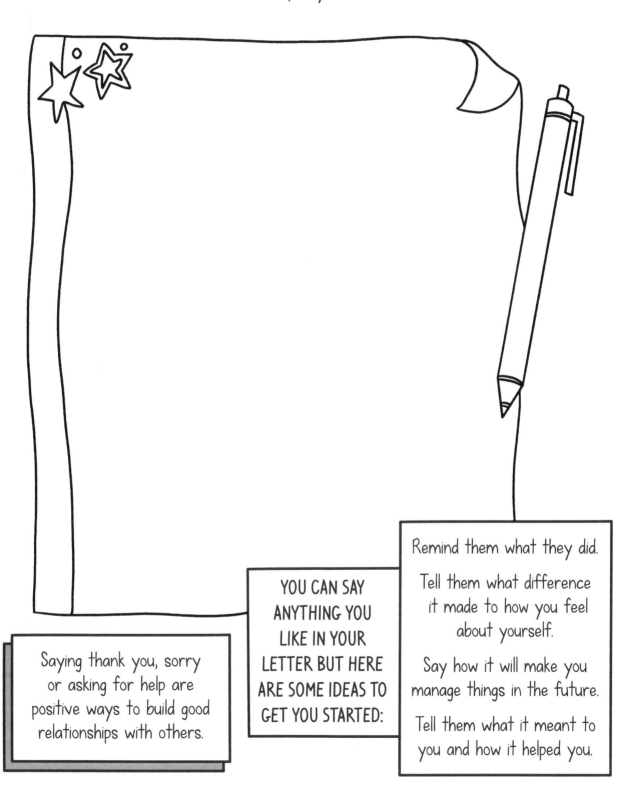

Saying thank you, sorry or asking for help are positive ways to build good relationships with others.

YOU CAN SAY ANYTHING YOU LIKE IN YOUR LETTER BUT HERE ARE SOME IDEAS TO GET YOU STARTED:

Remind them what they did.

Tell them what difference it made to how you feel about yourself.

Say how it will make you manage things in the future.

Tell them what it meant to you and how it helped you.

BODY POSITIVE

Some words just sound **SUPER** positive and bring you joy.

Colour this jumper while you enjoy the sight and sound of the words and how they make you feel.

KIND

HOPEFUL

GENEROUS

RESTED

PEACEFUL

MARVELLOUS

ENERGY

LOVED

HAPPY

STRONG

FRIENDS

COMFORTABLE

Fill this picture with your choice of words that you love to read, write or hear about yourself and see how they help you **BE POSITIVE!**

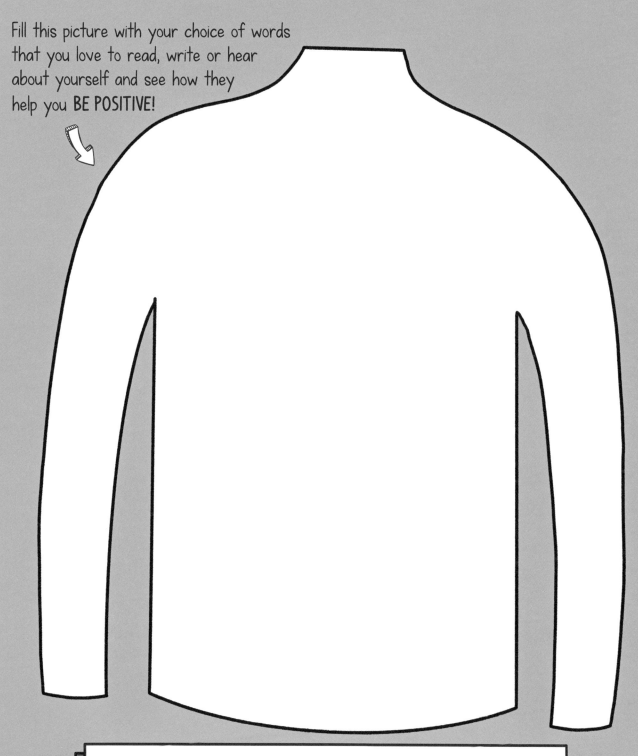

Why not come back to this picture and say a couple of the words to yourself next time you feel low or are being down on yourself?

TIME AFTER TIME

Write or draw a time when you were feeling confident and positive.

Really remember what you were thinking at the time as you do it.

This activity will rewire your brain to **BE POSITIVE!**

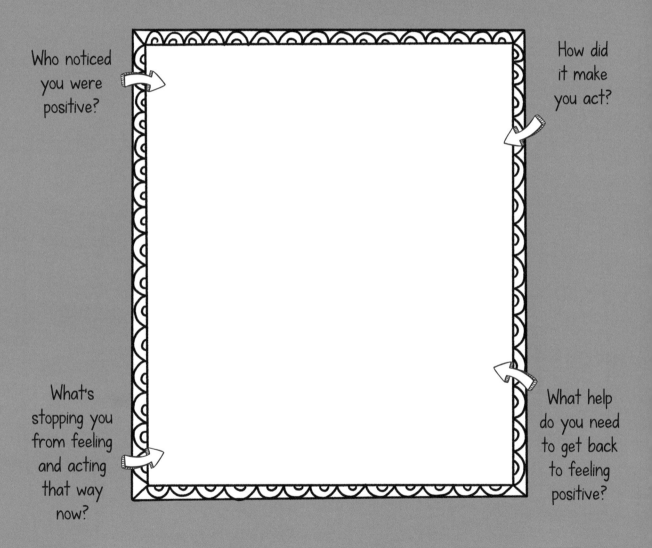

Who noticed you were positive?

How did it make you act?

What's stopping you from feeling and acting that way now?

What help do you need to get back to feeling positive?

Every time you feel your confidence slip or you find it hard to believe in yourself, come back to this page and get a boost!

IT'S ALL ABOUT YOU!

Fill this page with compliments that friends, family or adults give you about your personality, actions, kindness, skills, appearance – or anything else.

Keep coming back and writing them down as they happen.

Colour in the self-esteem battery as your confidence increases and keep coming back to read your compliments aloud to yourself until you believe them and can act more confidently because of them.

THINKING POINT:

Which compliments mean the most to you?

POSITIVE PEBBLES

I AM NOT ALONE

I AM LOVED

YOU WILL NEED:

- Pebbles
- Washing-up liquid
- Warm water
- Magazines or printed words
- Kitchen paper
- Scissors
- Sticky tape
- PVA glue and brush (if you want)

Collect a few medium-sized smooth pebbles from your garden or buy them from a craft store or garden centre.

Wash your pebbles and dry them completely on kitchen paper.

I BELIEVE IN ME

BE POSITIVE

Cut them out and stick them on the pebbles to create messages just for you.

Find words in magazines that are encouraging and positive or make your own list and print them.

Or you could give them to your friends as gifts, carefully choosing messages they would like.

To make them last longer, paint PVA glue over the top to varnish them with a shine.

GOOD ENOUGH

DETERMINED AND TALENTED

You could put them on your desk or a shelf, use them as paperweights or even a pen holder if you find one with a hole in it. If you find a piece of wood you could glue them on with hot glue and create a little collection.

Spend time reading your stones whenever you need to feel better or **BE POSITIVE!**

Make sure you ask an adult to help you with this activity!

NATURE WATCH

Spending time in nature is really good for your brain and body. It can slow your heart rate, reduce stress and develop your world view because you can't help but notice how amazing the world is.

YOU are part of the world – you're amazing too!

Go outside and look down. Find a living, growing or moving natural thing like an insect, a flower, a blade of grass or whatever you like.

Don't catch it or pick it – respect its right to be free and alive.

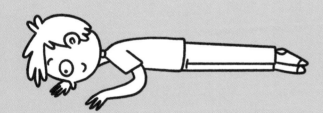

Sit or lay down and focus on watching your natural thing for one or two minutes (or longer if you like). Don't do anything except notice the thing you are looking at.

Look at it as if you are seeing it for the very first time.

Find two more things and repeat the activity.
When you've finished, notice the way you're feeling and describe it here:

SELFIES

Carry out small acts of kindness for people you care about and draw yourself doing them. Write about it if you prefer.

HERE ARE SOME IDEAS:

LET THEM GO BEFORE YOU

HOLD A DOOR OPEN

GIVE A COMPLIMENT

SAY HELLO TO SOMEONE NEW

HELP WITH
A CHORE

WRITE THEM A
NOTE OR A CARD

INVITE
SOMEONE NEW
TO PLAY

LET THEM HAVE
THE BEST BISCUIT

THINKING POINT:

What do you think your kindness
meant to the other person?

MASTERMIND

Now's your chance to shine.

Write 10 facts you know about something that interests you.

Spend time researching first or do it straight from memory if you prefer.

THE SUN IS 93 MILLION MILES FROM EARTH

BIRDS CAN'T LIVE IN SPACE

HIPPO MILK IS PINK

IT RAINS METAL ON VENUS

SPIDERS HAVE EIGHT LEGS

SNAILS CAN SLEEP FOR THREE YEARS

POSITIVE COLOURS

Fractals are a natural wonder – just like you.

They occur all over the world and in space.

COLOUR THESE
FRACTALS IN
POSITIVE,
BOLD COLOURS.

GOAL!

Set yourself a goal –
something you'd really like to
achieve in the next few weeks.

Maybe you'd like to try
something new or push yourself
with skills you already have.

WRITE IT HERE

VISUALISE yourself achieving it – make a mind movie of the
moment you get there. Watch it again and this time **LISTEN** to
how loudly your family and friends are celebrating your success.

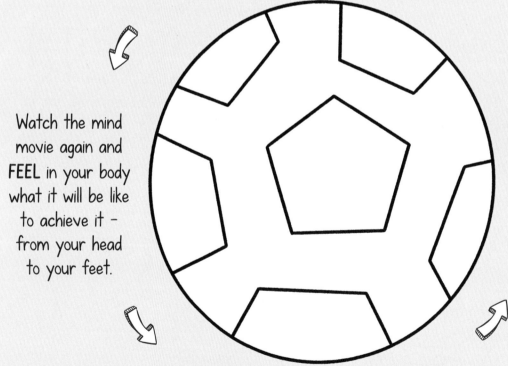

Watch the mind
movie again and
FEEL in your body
what it will be like
to achieve it –
from your head
to your feet.

BELIEVE you can
do this – you've
already rewired
your brain now
so you can be
sure it's possible.

BREATHE deeply in and out five times as
slowly as you can while you watch it again.

WHAT STEPS DO YOU NEED TO TAKE TO GET READY?
WRITE THEM ON THIS PAGE.

Get out there
and **GIVE** it a go!

You've rewired your brain
for success – well done! You can do this again every time you have a goal.
Why not set a goal for next month and next year?

YES YOU DO

I DESERVE LOVE

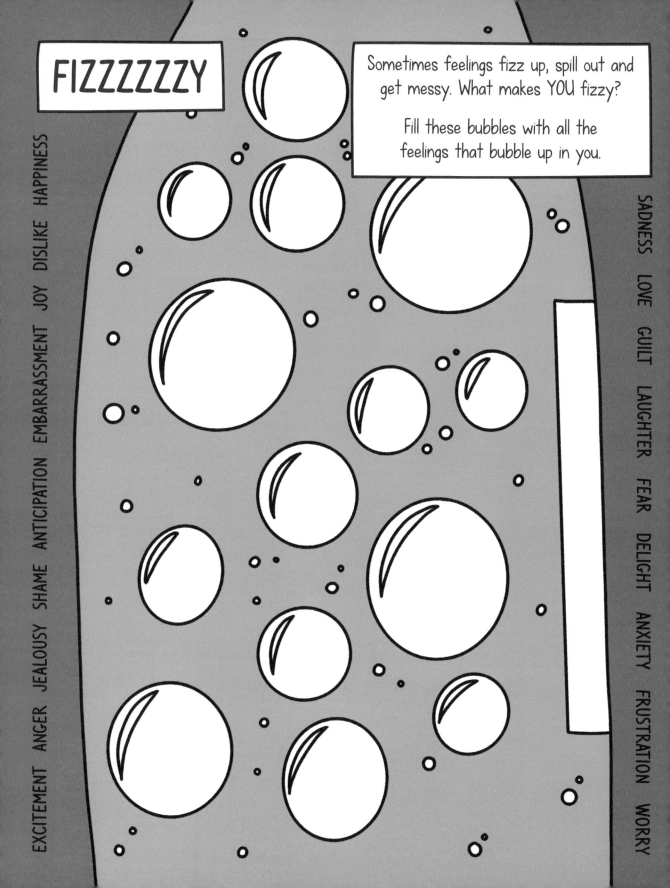

BLAST OFF!

People can say things that put you down or make you doubt yourself. It feels good to get those things blasting off into space and going away forever.

Fill this rocket with the things that get you fired up.

Then count down from 10 to zero.

Now BLAST OFF! and see and hear your rocket disappear out of the atmosphere.

Do you feel confident to challenge yourself to try something new for the first time?

What is it?

_____
_____
_____

Come back and give it a big tick when you've done it.

YOU'VE GOT THIS!

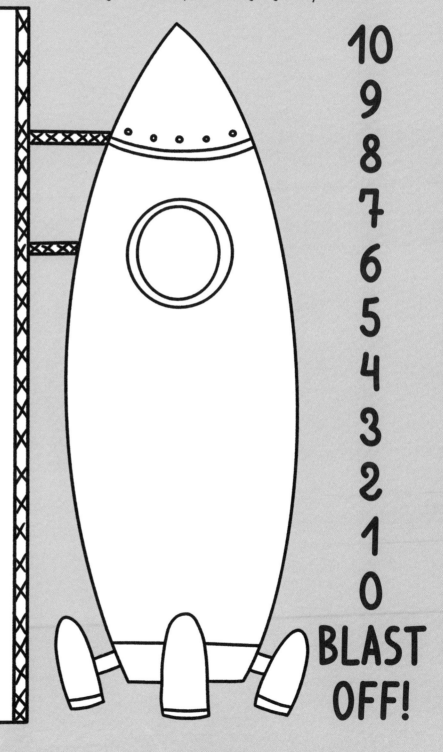

10
9
8
7
6
5
4
3
2
1
0
BLAST OFF!

FEED YOUR SOUL

Try this experiment to really notice what happens when you eat.

You might prefer to do it with a friend or adult.

YOU WILL NEED: • one raisin and • one you!

If you don't like raisins, use a blueberry, raspberry, blackcurrant or a very small piece of chocolate.

MAKE SURE IT'S SOMETHING YOU'RE NOT ALLERGIC TO!

HERE'S WHAT YOU DO:

Sit comfortably and take two or three deep breaths.

Place the raisin in your hand.

Look closely at the raisin with your full attention – imagine that it's like something from another planet that you've never seen before in your life.

Now close your eyes. Place the raisin on one of your fingers and gently move it around on your hand, exploring it carefully.

WHAT DOES THE RAISIN FEEL LIKE?

Hold the raisin near your nose and notice its smell.

Does anything interesting happen in your mouth or tummy.

 Slowly bring the raisin up to your mouth then rub it across your lips and notice what that feels like.

It might feel difficult not to just pop it in your mouth!

Put the raisin on your tongue and let it sit there for a few seconds. Don't chew it.

Just leave it on your tongue and notice how it feels.

Now very slowly begin to chew it. Bite it gently and notice what it feels like between your teeth.

Try not to swallow it just yet.

Wait until the taste fills your mouth, then swallow it down.

 Notice your breathing again and then open your eyes.

YOGA

STAR POSE

Try this Star Pose. It stretches your body in all directions at once.

Doing this pose with a steady and smooth breath will help you feel calm and will improve concentration.

Stretch your legs and feet wide apart, with your toes turned outwards. Keep your back, neck and head straight and stretch your arms in line with your shoulders with your hands above your feet. Hold and breathe calmly for a minute or two.

TILTED STAR POSE

If you have good balance you can tilt your star – start with the Star Pose, keeping one leg on the ground and then lower your shoulder on that side while you hold your other foot off the ground.

SPACE ROCKET POSE

This pose will make you feel positive, powerful and adventurous. Stand up tall and stretch out your spine.

Raise your hands above your head to create the nose of the spaceship.

Lift one foot a little way off the ground and rest it gently on top of the other foot.

Breathe calmly and enjoy the strength in your body. Now change feet and breathe calmly again.

FIVE LITTLE ALIENS

COLOUR IN THESE FIVE LITTLE
ALIENS HOWEVER YOU FANCY.

Which of these aliens do you
like the look of most? Why?

_____

_____

Now ask your friends or
family to say which ones
THEY like the look of most.

Does everyone like the
same one or different ones?

_____

_____

_____

THINKING POINT:

What do you notice first
about the way things look?

Check it out next time
you're out and about
and write it down here.

BLACK HOLE

Have you ever felt guilty, embarrassed or ashamed of something.

Maybe it was something someone else said or something you did.

You can learn from these feelings but you don't need to keep that old moment alive in your mind. You deserve forgiveness so now's the time to be kind to yourself and then move on.

Write it in this black hole and watch the universe crush it out of existence as you colour it all over as if it was never there.

You're free! It's gone! Life gets better from here. Notice how relieved and light you feel.

MAKE AMENDS

Give your body some love and care to make up for any mean things you've ever told it.

Put plasters over any part you've said unkind things to and write something positive about it to make amends and help it feel better.

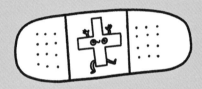

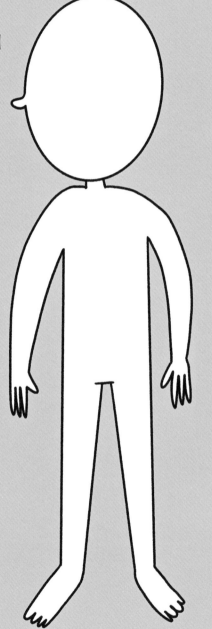

This activity will rewire your brain to be kinder to yourself.

NOW FIND SOMEONE YOU TRUST TO HAVE A LOVELY HUG AND FEEL BETTER ALL OVER.

SQUASH THE TOSH

You've got the power to change what you believe about yourself and how you feel.

Push your unhelpful, negative beliefs into this **TOSH SQUASHER** and see what helpful, positive ideas you can pull out of the other side

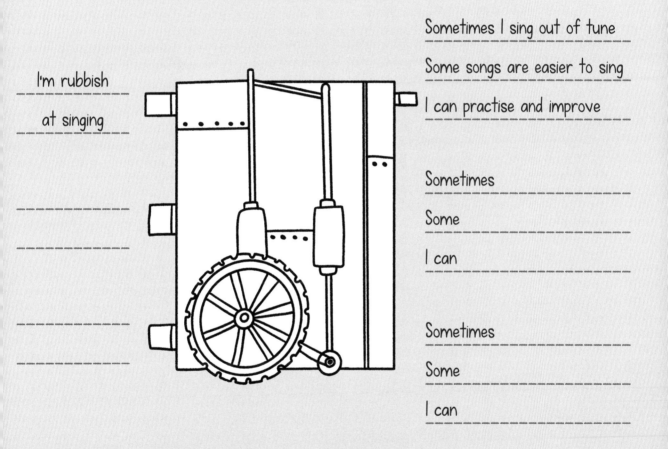

I'm rubbish
at singing

_____

_____

_____

_____

Sometimes I sing out of tune

Some songs are easier to sing

I can practise and improve

Sometimes _____

Some _____

I can _____

Sometimes _____

Some _____

I can _____

Try using your **BE POSITIVE!** power on two of your negative beliefs.

Whenever you feel rubbish, you know what to do to change how you feel. **SQUASH THE TOSH!**

MOONWALK

Put on your favourite tunes and dance like a visitor from a distant planet.

Teach an Earthling a new dance that you've invented. Make up your own moves and swing those arms, hands, hips, legs and feet – in fact, use every bit of you! Do your own thing – **THERE ARE NO RULES!**

Get your friends and family joining in.

You never know, you could start the next dance craze!

GLITTERY GALAXY

Sometimes everything feels huge.

Focus your attention and bring it all down to a more manageable size with this glittery galaxy jar.

Fill your jar or bottle about half the way with warm water.

Add the glitter glue then add glitter.

Next, add a few drops f food colouring or a

Close the jar or bottle. You can seal the lid with glue for extra protection.

SHAKE!!!

Watch as the glitter settles. This will help your feelings to settle too.

RESPECT YOURSELF

Know yourself to respect yourself.

Fill in these frames with the things that matter to you.

MY HOPES

Values are what you expect from yourself and others, like kindness, honesty, fairness, trust, loyalty, respect.

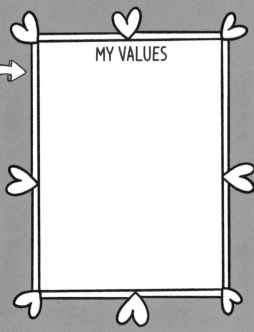

MY VALUES

Hopes are what you wish for yourself, the people you love and the world around you.

BE TRUE TO YOURSELF AT ALL TIMES.

Beliefs are the things that you hold true, have faith or confidence in and are important to you.

MY DREAMS

Dreams are the things you would love to do or be part of.

MY BELIEFS

BOUNDARIES

You deserve respect. If you feel unhappy with how some people treat you, it can affect your self-esteem and your confidence.

You can set boundaries and make decisions about what you're comfortable with in a relationship. If someone is mean to you or leaves you out, you don't have to put up with it. You can ask them to stop and involve a trusted adult if they don't.

I EXPECT PEOPLE TO BE POLITE

I DESERVE HONESTY

I DESERVE KINDNESS

Draw or write how you want to be treated in these planets. Use your own ideas or choose some of the examples. Colour in the boundaries around them.

THINKING POINT:

When you feel left out it can hurt as much as a physical injury. Think about a time you felt left out or a time you left someone else out. What did it feel like?

GROW YOUR OWN

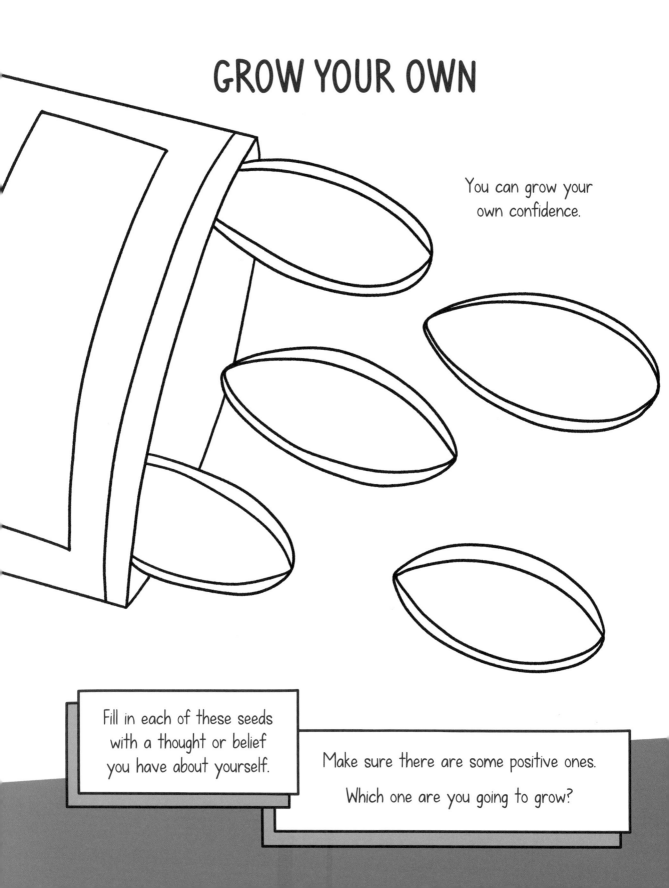

You can grow your own confidence.

Fill in each of these seeds with a thought or belief you have about yourself.

Make sure there are some positive ones.

Which one are you going to grow?

THE ONE YOU FEED IS THE ONE THAT WILL GROW!

Take the seed you'd most like to get rid of and plant it in this pot without soil, air, water or light.

Write its name on the label.

Watch it give up and wither away without anything to feed it.

Find two seeds that really need a chance to grow to help you act more confidently. Plant them in these pots and write on the labels.

Cover them in soil, water them and give them plenty of sunlight.

Colour the picture if you like.

Keep coming back to check their progress every time you use this book. As you feel the beliefs growing inside you, draw the stem, leaves and flowers on and colour them in.

When you've grown this strong and healthy belief, what new challenge will you try to test it out?

_____

_____

_____

Come back and give it a big tick when you've done the challenge:

MIRROR STICKERS

Make sure you ask an adult before you stick anything on your mirrors.

What do you see when you look in the mirror?

Draw your reflection.

What do you feel, think or believe about your reflection?

What do you feel, think or believe about yourself?

I see _____

I am _____

My reflection looks _____

After two weeks, come back and describe how different you feel and what has changed about the way you act.

_____
_____
_____

Colour in these double-sided mirror stickers and cut them out carefully.

Stick them with sticky tack on all your mirrors to remind yourself how awesome you are whenever you look at yourself.

I AM THE ONE AND ONLY

Everybody's body is unique. Including yours.

Which parts of your body and appearance make you happy?

I like my _____

I love my _____

I respect my _____

I value my _____

My _____ is awesome.

My _____ is wonderful.

THINKING POINT:

What is one thing you wish people knew about you?

STUCK ON YOU

Have you had any sticky moments?

Other people's words and actions can stick to you and keep bothering you.

It's hard to get rid of them.

Stand in this warm rain and enjoy watching them all unstick from you and wash away.

They can dissolve and go into the earth to help beautiful plants and trees to grow.

Write what they were in the raindrops.

You can start fresh now - they aren't stuck on you anymore so you're free to enjoy your rewired, clear mind.

SAY WHAT?

Megan the Koala and her friends are comparing themselves to each other.

They feel sad because their friends can do things they can't, and they all look so different.

What would you say to help them **BE POSITIVE!** and to remind them they are awesome just as they are?

_____

_____

_____

_____

I can't play hide and seek.

I'm no good at swimming.

My beak is too big.

My tail is too small.

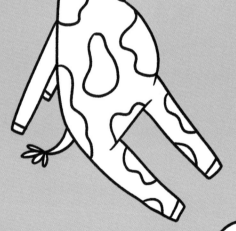

I can't climb trees.

I can't cuddle my friends.

I'm too furry.

My claws are too long.

COLOUR THIS IN

I'M NOT PERFECT

BUT I'M GOOD ENOUGH!

KINDNESS CAPSULE

We all need to feel looked after and loved.

Make yourself a kindness capsule for those days when you're not feeling on top of the world.

Decorate it however you wish with paint, wrapping paper (old comics make excellent wrapping paper!), fabric and ribbons, old posters, magazine pictures – anything that takes your fancy.

YOU WILL NEED:

- A shoebox or something similar (old lunchboxes or ice-cream boxes work well)

Fill your capsule with items that will make you happy when you're sad, calm when you're anxious and busy when you're bored.

Why not make a kindness capsule for a friend, too?

HERE ARE SOME IDEAS:

- soft toys
- modelling clay
- your favourite collector card or toy

- stress ball
- fidget toys
- friendship bracelets

- old ticket
- blowing bubbles
- a small mirror for pulling faces at yourself

- positive pebbles
- beads
- photos

- puzzle book
- highlighters
- old birthday cards from special people

CLOUD FLYING

Look at this fluffy cloud.

Draw yourself floating on it feeling completely relaxed, safe and comfortable.

Imagine, draw and colour the landscape below your cloud.

Your cloud can take you over rivers and lakes, fields and forests, dancing dolphins in sparkling seas, snowy, white mountains or sizzling deserts. Wherever you want to go.

Spend five minutes imagining yourself calmly and gently flying over your landscape, as if you're really there.

HOW DOES IT FEEL?

If you enjoy this, come back to your cloud whenever you need or want to.

Play some lovely music while you do it if you like.

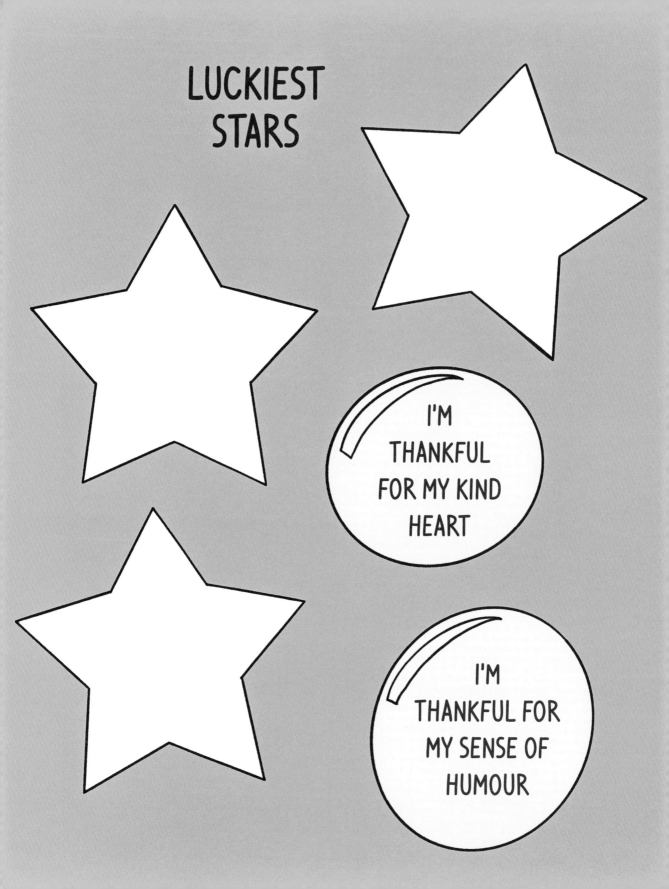

Fill in these lucky stars and bubbles with the things about yourself that you're thankful for.

I'M THANKFUL
FOR MY SKILL AT
_____

You can also ask your family, friends
and loved ones for ideas or ask them to fill in
some stars for you. Add more stars if you want to.

SPACE UNICORNS

We all feel sorry for ourselves and have negative thoughts from time to time.

You might think:

EVERYONE'S PICKING ON YOU

BAD THINGS ONLY HAPPEN TO YOU

PEOPLE WANT TO UPSET YOU

EVERYONE IS MEAN AND UNKIND

You need the space unicorns to help you **BE POSITIVE!**

They've got a few questions for you to answer.

Try them out every time you feel sorry for yourself and rewire your brain to question your negative thoughts.

You can write down your ideas if it helps.

When things feel really tricky, ask an adult you trust to go through these questions with you.

Then take time for a **TALK 12** together.

Have a hug too. You deserve it!

Talk to someone for 12 minutes about anything you like – comics, books, hobbies, sports, fashion, animals, music and films all make for good conversations.

TALK 12

What's made you feel this way?

_____
_____
_____

Is it true?

_____

What are you basing this on?

_____
_____
_____

Could there be another explanation for what is happening?

_____
_____
_____

Space unicorns can catch your negative thoughts and trap them forever – why not help them?

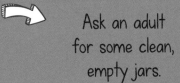

Ask an adult for some clean, empty jars.

Write your negative thoughts on pieces of paper and trap them inside the jars.

Store them in the dark somewhere or ask someone to put them out of the way in a high cupboard or in a shed.

MISSION POSSIBLE

Some things we can change, and some things we can't. And sometimes we have to learn to live with things we don't like.

It's much easier to do this when you can BE POSITIVE! Keep going – you can do it!

List three things you can change, three things you can't change and three things that will change in time.

A MILLION DREAMS

Fill in these dream bubbles with lovely memories you have of people, places, pets, parties and picnics.

Or absolutely any lovely memory you like. Save some for your future memories if you want. You could add words, drawings or even photographs.

Why not tell someone about them, describing in as much detail as you can how you felt at the time?

SHOOT FOR THE MOON

We all need to get a good nights' sleep.

If you're too tired in the daytime, it's hard to **BE POSITIVE!**

Here are some things you might need for a good night.

A DRINK

FAVOURITE TEDDY

A LIGHT SNACK

LISTEN TO A RELAXATION CD

LISTEN TO A BEDTIME STORY

A HUG

Make your own personal list of what YOU need to sleep tight:

NIGHT LIGHT

WARM SOCKS

QUIET

Imagine putting on a spacesuit when you put on your PJs so you can quickly go off to sleep and dream about your next mission. If you've got things on your mind, get the space unicorns to pop in and clear your worries away.

As you lie in bed, why not try the breathing exercises from earlier in the book?

HERE'S A REMINDER FOR 3:5 BREATHING

Get comfortable. Notice your body breathing in and out.

After a few breaths, start to count along with yourself, making your in-breath last for the count of three and your out-breath last for the count of five, breathing smoothly.

Draw yourself tucked up all cosy and sleeping calmly all night long.

HIGH FIVE

Keep your body and brain healthy and happy every day with a high five!

LEARN HOW BY FILLING IN THE MISSING WORDS:

WATER

ENJOY

HEALTH

ENOUGH

1. Eat for _____ .

2. Drink _____ .

3. Get plenty of _____ .

4. Get _____ rest and sleep.

5. Make sure every day has space to do things you _____ with people who care about you.

EXERCISE

1. health   2. water   3. exercise   4. enough   5. enjoy

TOP TIPS

Our friends need us as much as we need them.

If your friend's self-esteem battery needs charging up with **BE POSITIVE!** power, what advice would you offer?

Make a **BE POSITIVE! TOP TIPS** poster.

THINKING POINT:

Look through this book for ideas and to see which activities you've found the most helpful.

CHECK-IN & BLAST OFF

Now you've learnt how to **BE POSITIVE!** it's time to check-in on your battery power.

SELF-ESTEEM

I respect myself for who I am.

There are things I do well and things I need to improve.

I feel proud of my efforts.

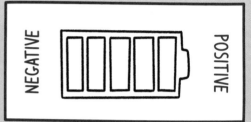

SELF-CONFIDENCE

I try things even if I might not succeed.

I am confident to challenge myself.

It's always worth trying to do my best.

BODY IMAGE

My body can do all kinds of brilliant things.

I can learn new skills.

There are things I like about my appearance.

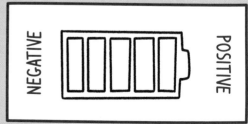

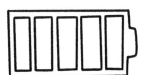

NEGATIVE | POSITIVE

Good things do happen.

Some people are really kind.

I can have fun and go to interesting places.

Compare the power in your batteries now with the ones at the start of the book.

What has improved?

What do you need to keep working at?

Don't forget you can go back and do any of these activities again, as often as you like.

THINKING POINT:

Challenge yourself to try one new thing now you know how to **BE POSITIVE!**

Write it down with any steps you need to think about to get there:

YOU'RE AMAZING!
TRUST YOURSELF

IT'S TIME TO BLAST OFF! GO YOU!

THE BIT FOR GROWN UPS

This activity book is perfect for parents, carers, teachers, learning mentors, therapists, social workers and youth leaders who want to help children to believe in themselves and others and develop positive body image, self-esteem and confidence.

Modern life bombards children with ideals of success, popularity and perfection alongside the everyday message to be better and do better as they grow, make mistakes and learn. Internal and external pressures can cause them to compare themselves with others and feel they aren't good enough which damages confidence in themselves, their developing bodies and the world around them.

Children may become overwhelmed and struggle to make sense of what is happening without the language or tools to explain their distress. You might notice an increase in self-doubt and negative thoughts, along with complaints of tummy aches, headaches or tiredness and avoidance of previously enjoyed activities.

In a loving and nurturing environment, children are resilient and will often work through problems without needing additional help. This book enables your child to explore, express and explain their self-doubts and open up the conversation with you. The fun activities increase positivity, confidence, self-esteem and self-belief, build further resilience, combat negative thoughts and expectations and encourage a heathy sense of themselves and their world.

If your child's lack of confidence persists beyond three months or escalates rather than decreases, talk to their school, your GP, a counsellor or one of the organisations listed below for support and guidance.

YOUNG MINDS PARENT HELPLINE

Mon-Fri 9.30 a.m. to 4 p.m. – free in England, Scotland, Wales and Northern Ireland.

Call to talk through your child's problem. Advisers will listen to your concerns and questions in complete confidentiality, help you to understand your child's behaviour and give you practical advice on where to go next. If you need further help, they'll refer you to a specialist e.g. psychotherapist, psychiatrist, psychologist or mental health nurse within seven days.

Tel: 0808 802 5544   www.youngminds.org.uk

MIND – FOR BETTER MENTAL HEALTH

Mind's team provides information on a range of topics including: types of mental health problems, where to get help, medication and alternative treatments and advocacy.

They will look for details of help and support in your own area.

Call weekdays 9 a.m. to 6 p.m., Phone calls from UK landlines are charged at local rates. Charges from mobile telephones vary considerably.

Tel: 0300 123 3393   Text: 86463
www.mind.org.uk

SANE HELPLINE

SANE's helpline is a national, seven days a week, out-of-hours (6 p.m. to 11 p.m.) telephone helpline for anyone coping with mental illness, including concerned relatives or friends.

Tel: 0300 304 7000
www.sane.org.uk

DR. SHARIE COOMBES